To Benjamin
Happy 8th Birthday
Lots of love
Gill, David
Catherine & William
xx.

CREEPY POEMS

Illustrated by Stephen Cartwright

Selected by Heather Amery

Poems by

Dave Calder, Tony Charles, Stanley Cook, Gina Douthwaite,
Gavin Ewart, John Foster, David Harmer, Libby Houston, Michael Johnson,
Julie O'Callaghan, Kevin McCann, Robin Mellor, Trevor Millum,
Judith Nicholls, Irene Rawnsley, Vernon Scannell, Anthony Smith,
Sue Stewart, Marian Swinger and Charles Thomson.

With thanks to Lois Beeson

Tell Me It Isn't

Try not to stare
But tell me – that shadow there
With its head in the air
Isn't a bear . . .
There isn't a bear
Come out of its lair
At the top of the stair,
IS there??

Take care how you speak,
But – tell me, that creak,
It isn't the creak of the freak,
The flying freak
With the crooked beak
About to sneak
Up from behind,
IS it??

Tell me that sound
Isn't the sound of the hound,
The red-eyed hound
Creeping around
Dribbling and crunching
The bones it found
About to leap with one bound
On my back!
(It isn't, is it?)

Tell me – the movement I saw
Behind the door . . .
It wasn't a paw
It wasn't a claw
It wasn't the Beast
About to roar
And pounce and gnaw – WAS IT??

Yes, I know you told me before
But I'm still not sure,
So . . . tell me *once* more.

Trevor Millum

The Ancient Horrors

I met an ancient Vampire once
whilst ambling on the heath:
the bloodbank had to give him blood –
he'd lost his new false teeth.

I met an ancient Hagwitch once:
her home help came each day
to bring her beetle juice and toast
with frogs' legs on a tray.

I met an ancient Werewolf once
who said, "you'll do for tea,"
but he was in a wheelchair, so
he didn't frighten me.

I met an ancient Ghostie once
who seemed quite out of breath;
he tried to make a moaning sound
and coughed himself to death.

I met an ancient Monster once
who lived around Loch Ness,
but she was only one foot high
(she'd shrunk with age I guess).

I met an ancient Zombie once:
he sent me into fits,
for when he went to grab my arm
he promptly fell to bits.

Marian Swinger/Charles Thomson

The Hoover Spook

A naughty spook named Norman Head
sneaked in and hid beneath a bed.

Then, while the owners dozed inside,
he lurked amidst the dust and spied

until a sleepy leg hung out,
grabbed hold with an excited shout

and caused the couple so much fright
their hair went absolutely white.

Next day the trembling couple said,
"Let's vacuum underneath the bed.

If anything is hiding there
we'll give it an almighty scare."

Next moment Norman gave a wail
to find himself amidst a gale,

he clung in panic to a spring,
he lost his grasp, there was a PING!,

with bulging eyes and frenzied shout
he vanished up the vacuum spout.

A prisoner in the Hoover bag
with spiders, dust and half a fag,

poor Norman brooded hard and long
on making the machine go wrong.

That night the Hoover gave a roar
and spread its contents on the floor.

Encouraged by this great success
in manufacturing a mess

(on which a spook's good name depends)
he notified his ghostly friends,

"Don't waste your time beneath a bed –
frequent a Hoover bag instead."

So if your Hoover splurts out dust,
don't look inside unless you must.

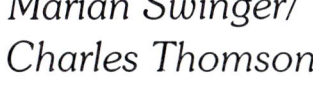

It's almost certain, if you do,
a horrid spook will yell out "BOO!!!"

Marian Swinger/
Charles Thomson

Willy Was a Wizard

Willy was a Wizard
who could never spell it right:
tried to fix a thunderstorm –
got the sun at night;
tried to paint his top hat black –
ended up with white;
couldn't even scare a flea
or give a mouse a fright;
SPELLS FOR ALL, the notice said,
but that was there in *spite*
of Willy being a Wizard
who *couldn't* get it right!

Judith Nicholls

5

Mary Celeste

On the Atlantic Ocean
The light winds blow
And the abandoned ship
Tacks crazily to and fro.

Safe and sound,
The ship sails on;
Only the lifeboat
And people are gone.

One of the hatches
Is lying open
But the cargo's intact
And nothing's missing or broken.

No sign why the crew,
The captain, his child and wife
Should suddenly panic
And flee for dear life.

No signs of a struggle to be seen,
But a letter left half-written
And a reel of cotton and a thimble
In place on the sewing machine.

Tins of food seized from the store,
But the captain's watch on its hook
Pipes left and tobacco
And jewels and trinkets in a drawer.

On the Atlantic ocean
The light winds blow
And the abandoned ship
Tacks crazily to and fro.

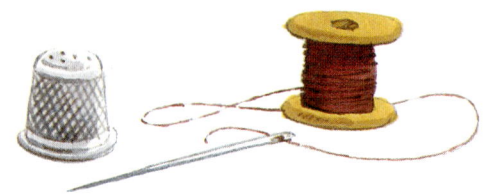

Stanley Cook

The Room Went Cold

The room went cold
and I felt something
like a sticky hand
creep along my neck
and down my spine.

It trickled down my leg
stroked my foot
then slid off my toe
and on to the floor.

I stared with one eye
I stared with two eyes
I got my magnifying glass
and my dad's binoculars
and my sister's ruler
and the kitchen scales

so I could see it
measure it
weigh it

but there was

nothing to see

nothing to measure

nothing to weigh

nothing to be
frightened of

was there?

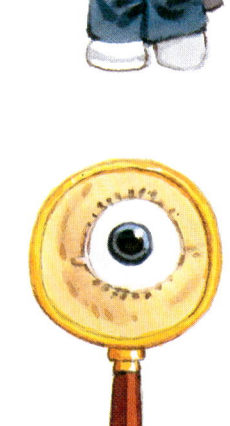

Sue Stewart

Fearless

Ghosts and foul ghoulies
I can withstand;
skeletons, witches,
I'd take by the hand.
A poltergeist's welcome,
a dragon is grand
BUT . . .

Dinosaurs, Krakens –
such friendly ways!
Octopus, jellyfish,
Martians from space.
The Centaur, a phoenix
I'd look in the face
BUT . . .

Who'll move the spider?

Who'll move the spider?

Judith Nicholls

7

What's There?

Raging, crazily, round the roof
as though in torture from a tooth
this uninvited guest gyrates,
cracks creaking beams, whips under slates,
prises open trapdoor jaws,
pads across cold bedroom floors,
rattles handles,
battles
with doors,

hides in curtains, whines and s-i-g-h-s,
traces flesh with fingers of ice,
SCREAMS down chimneys, *startling* flames.
Hear breathless voices wailing names?
hoaxing, coaxing from the stair,
calling cats who bristle hair,
cower and yowl
at what – ?
What's there

raging, crazily, round the roof?

They say they know – but where's the proof?

Gina Douthwaite

8

Dracula's Complaint

You'd look poorly, you'd look pale
Skin all deathly shades of grey
You'd look sickly, you'd look frail
Stuck in a coffin in a grave all day.

Go for a shave but I can't see my face
Spend half my life dressed up as a bat
Living all my days at a subnormal pace
With these enormous teeth, who needs that?

Night after night I ride my bike
Looking around for a bite to eat
Living in a graveyard isn't what I like
The neighbours howl, their breath's not sweet.

I'm bored stiff, it's a pain in the neck
Living in the ground, cold and damp
I'm turning into a Transylvanian wreck
My whole life needs a thorough re-vamp.

I look in the paper, read the small ads
I need a new job, need a fresh start
I want to escape the curse of the Vlads
Try to do that with a stake through your heart.

David Harmer

Grandma's Dream

This is the dream that Grandma saw.
The dream came back year after year

Always the same – like a film – she said:
She was going along a country road,

Along the road and in at the gates
(Horses' heads on the weather-worn posts),

In at the gates and down the drive
(A yellow tower from a dark grove),

Down the drive and up to the door
(Tracks in the gravel like a turning car's

But no car nor cart nor carriage now),
By the shallow steps in the glaring view

Of thirty-five windows (blank as water
In an old canal in a summer shadow)

And over the threshold and into the hall
(From the gilded ceiling the air hung still).

No one challenged her, no voice spoke,
No cough, no footstep, rustle nor click.

Corkscrew pillars of clouded marble –
Between them stood a massive table

Covered, in all that solemn splendour,
With rubbish – more than she ever remembered –

Like screwed-up papers grey with grease,
Green-flecked bread with a half-chewed slice,

Snot-glued tissues, slimy skin,
Curd-smeared bottles and a fallen beam,

Tea-bags, coke cans – Grandma stared.
Beyond the hearth a shadow stirred:

A dark arched door began to open
For a girl with a tray, in a long apron.

The girl saw Grandma in her dream,
Dropped the tray with a wild scream
And flung her apron up over her face –

She always woke at the same place.

Grandma's dream. Or was Grandma a ghost
For a real girl somewhere in a real house?

Libby Houston

Faith

There was a young lady of Ryde,
Who was carried too far by the tide;
    A man-eating shark
    Said: "How's this for a lark?
I knew that the Lord would provide."

Anon

11

Assembly

I don't want to see any racing in the corridor,
a gentle glide's what we expect in here;
not that I mind a little heavy-handed fear
but you high spirits must slow down.

And I've had complaints that some of you
slip out at playtime. Let it be quite clear
that you stay in the graveyard till you hear
the bell. The chippy's out of bounds,
so is the sweetshop and your other favourite haunts.
I'll stop your little fun and groans:
there'll be a year's detention in the dungeon
for anyone caught chewing anything but bones.

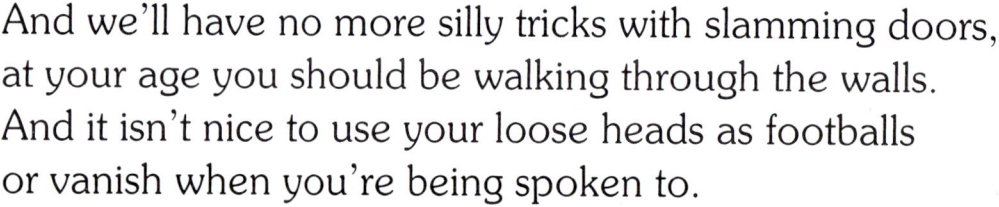

And we'll have no more silly tricks with slamming doors,
at your age you should be walking through the walls.
And it isn't nice to use your loose heads as footballs
or vanish when you're being spoken to.

And finally, I really must remind you
that moans are not allowed before midnight
especially near the staff-room. It's impolite
and disturbs the creatures – I mean teachers –
resting in despair and mournful gloom.
You there – stop wriggling in your coffin, I can't
bear to see a scruffy ghost –
put your face back where it was this instant
or you won't get to go howling at the moon.

Class Three, instead of double Shrieking
you'll do Terminal Disease with Dr. Cyst;
Class Two stays here for Creepy Sneaking.
The rest of you can go. School dismissed.

Dave Calder

What My Father Said

"Great Aunt Alice used to live
in a coffin,"
my father said,
"But was she dead?"
I asked,
"Oh no," he replied,
"At least, I don't think so."

"Old Uncle Jerome never had
a home,"
my father said,
"But used to wander
the streets alone with
a sack on his head.
He's dead."

"Your mother's brother,"
my father said,
"Had a bit of bother with
a sliced loaf of bread."
"Yes?" I asked,
"Yes," my father said.

My father said
"Just look at the time.
Come on,
up the wooden hill
it's just a short climb.
Off you go to bed."

But I can't sleep
and I'm thinking still,
should I believe
what my father said?

Robin Mellor

13

Why Are We Hiding?

Why are we hiding in here?
Why are we hiding in here?
What's up? What's there? What makes you stare?
Why are we hiding in here?

Why are we hiding in here?
Is it that breathing noise coming near –
Is that the thing I've got to fear?

Why are we hiding in here?
Is it that shape that's begun to appear –
Is that the thing I've got to fear?

Why are we hiding in here?
Is it that outline becoming clear –
Is that the thing I've got to fear?

DON'T tell me that there's nothing to fear
I KNOW there's something coming near
And NOTHING you say will make it disappear
OH – WHY are we hiding in here?

Trevor Millum

Creepy

Ghosts and goblins don't strike me as creepy –
If anything, they bore me and make me feel sleepy.
I know they're not real – more like a bad dream.
It's the *real* Creepy-Crawlies that make *me* scream!

Gavin Ewart

14

The Ghost

You may have to wait for hours
For a bus or a train
Or wait the whole of the year
For Christmas to come again.

But the hundreds of years
The ghost had to wait
Have almost worn him away
And he is thin and his voice is faint.

He has worn out the home he had
When once he was alive
And only a few battered ruins
From the walls of his castle survive.

He has grown as pale
As a gleam of moonlight
Coming through a gap in the curtains
As the old church clock strikes midnight.

Don't try to seize him –
He is thin as a shadow;
Listen carefully –
His voice is faint as an echo.

He is so worn out
You hardly know he is there
When he passes you by
In a gust of ice-cold air.

Stanley Cook

Camping Out

Can we sleep out in the tent, Dad?
Go on, just him and me!
It's a full moon,
not a cloud in sight!
We'll be quiet as
mice when the cat's about –
oh, *please* let us stay the night?

You can pitch your tent down
*   the garden*
by the lilac, or just behind;
but mind you're in by midnight
if you're going to change your mind.
The key will be out till twelve,
but not a second more.
I don't want prowlers after that –
at twelve I lock the door!

Great Dad!
We'll be out till morning –
you've never let us before!
We'll fetch all we need
before it's dark
then you can lock your door.

The key will be out till twelve,
I said, but not a second more!

Now, what do we need?
Water, jug,
toothpaste, mug,
towel, rug,
toothbrush
    . . .

Since when were you so keen
on keeping clean?

You can't camp out down
    the Amazon
without the proper gear.
We could be here a *year*,
exploring dark Brazil
until – who knows?

All right, a torch then,
I suppose. Sleeping bags.
Pillows?

There's no room.
Mosquito nets come first,
and books to read
by torch or moon.
Pencils, notebooks.
Sweaters – two at least.
And don't forget the
    midnight feast!

What do explorers eat?
Will crisps and apples do,
with peanut-butter sandwiches,
bananas, orange juice,
and baked beans for the stew?

They'll do!
    . . .

I wish we'd brought a pillow.
It's really dark.
I thought you said no cloud?
Should we close the flap –
to keep mosquitoes out, I mean?

Or leopards!

. . . and to keep us warm.
There goes that flash again.
The air feels heavy.
P'rhaps a jungle storm?
Listen!
Can you hear – a breeze?
Something's rustling,
quickly, *freeze!*

*Could it be
some deadly snake,
uncoiling for . . .*

For goodness sake,
it's only trees!
Why are we whispering?

*Oh, look!
What IS that shadow up above?
I'm sure I saw it move!*

It's nothing,
just the lilac.
Or some bat or owl
out on the prowl
for supper too.

TOOWHIT, TOOWHOO!

No need to jump,
it's nearer me than you!

*I didn't jump!
What time is it,
only five to midnight?
Just wondered.
Thought it might be more.*

I DON'T WANT PROWLERS AFTER THAT,
AT TWELVE I LOCK THE DOOR! . . .

*Aren't you cold?
I wish we'd brought more blankets,
the jungle's not so hot
when sun's gone down;
we didn't think of that.*

Not cold, just hungry.
It's great out here,
but as for food –
we should have brought much more.
Explorers need their sustenance.
Another time, we'll plan it better . . .

But meantime,
RACE YOU TO THE DOOR!

Judith Nicholls

Under the Bedclothes

What is it walking outside in the dark?
Is it the ghost of poor Mollie Park,
who lived all alone with the spiders and rats?
– *Cover your ears and pretend it's just cats!*

What is it tapping the window so gently?
Is it the ghost of poor Johnny Bentley,
Who fell off a cliff when no-one was near?
– *Cover your ears and pretend you can't hear!*

What is it dripping downstairs in the kitchen?
Is it the ghost of poor Billy Ditchen,
Who drowned with his dog in the cold grey stream?
– *Cover your ears and pretend it's a dream!*

What is it creaking upstairs so slowly?
Is it the ghost of poor Mollie Coley,
With old tattered clothing and twigs in her hair?
– *Cover your ears and pretend she's not there!*

What is it opening the bedroom door
And moving so softly across the floor?
– *Cover your ears, and close your eyes tight,
And just hope that it's Mum come to see you're all right!*

Tony Charles

Who's Afraid?

Do I have to go haunting tonight?
The children might give me a fright.
It's dark in that house.
I might meet a mouse.
Do I have to go haunting tonight?

I don't like the way they scream out,
When they see me skulking about.
I'd much rather stay here,
Where there's nothing to fear.
Do I have to go haunting tonight?

John Foster

The Follower

Hiding like a tree cat
in a dappled cave of leaves,
watching like a kestrel
soaring high above the eaves,

Stalking as a grey wolf
through the misty heather,
stealthy as a wily fox
scenting fur or feather,

Padding close as tigers
to the edges of your mind,
whose the footsteps following?

Dare you look behind?

Irene Rawnsley

The Gloom

What waits?
Up the dark alley,
Knife sharp and glinting,
Cooking pot ready.

What lives?
Inside the chimney,
Moaning and howling,
Calling down thunder.

THE GLOOM!

What hides?
Under the wardrobe,
Licking its fat chops,
Grabbing at ankles.

What moves?
Invisibly through you,
Creaking the floorboards,
Making you shudder.

THE GLOOM!

What haunts?
Old empty houses,
Overgrown graveyards,
Your very worst dream.

But what runs?
When you make up a poem,
Blow a loud raspberry
Then sing a daft song.

THE GLOOM!

Kevin McCann

Cooked

A careless old cook of Saltash
In her second-hand car had a crash;
   She drove through a wall,
   House, garden and all,
And ended up Banger-and-Mash.

Anon

Silas Scale's Piano

Silas Scale left in his will
an instrument that can't keep still.

With phantom fingers on the keys
it strikes out quavers, semibreves,
and renders rondos, unrequested.

Such mechanism must be tested!
Silas Scale's piano's front

was purposely removed to hunt
for tiny paw marks in the dust –
the answer to the mystery must

be found in mice abseiling wires,
or twanging chords to tune up choirs

for mousical productions of
Shaketail's "Cheese – The Food We Love".
. . . No Phily-monic escapades

nor older-rodent matinees
had taken place, which quite perturbed –

dust lay too deep and undisturbed
for mousy-style participation.
No hand had they. What implication?

Scale's piano held no clue yet
yesterday it played a duet

enchanting all who heard this vital,
truly spirited recital
from Silas Scale's piano.

Gina Douthwaite

21

Dusk Jockey

Good evening, everyone.
Let me remind you who I am.
I am not your favourite man.
You've never seen me but you know my voice.
The tunes I play make none of you rejoice:
They're what you'd call decidedly unpop.
The only charts that they'd be sure to top
Would be a list of sounds you most detest.
Now and then I bring along a guest
To give my programme added interest:
I had a vampire in the studio
No longer than half-an-hour ago
But he was thirsty and he had to go.
He says he hopes he'll visit some of you
For one quick drink before the night is through.
If you're anaemic you can sleep quite tight
Except a news flash filtered through last night:
A madman has infected all supplies
Of water everywhere. Perhaps all lies,
But I wouldn't bet on it if I were you.
And now a card from Mr Pettigrew
Who says he's looking forward keenly to
The funeral of Mrs Pettigrew.
Some music now for Mrs Thumb and Tom –
The Zombies' March and Lepers' Chorus from
An opera whose title slips my mind.

And then I've got to go, before the blind
Of total night comes down. But don't believe I'm through:
Dusk is the time I find most work to do.
I've got to groom my mount while there's still light;
I'll ride my mare into your sleep tonight.

Vernon Scannell

Spider Night

Darkness
has too many legs,
walks high and silently
across wide spaces
into everywhere;

spreads hands
like spider webs
across your garden,
your house,
your room;

watches
through the long night
with unsleeping
spiders' eyes;

hears you breathing.

Irene Rawnsley

Ode to a Nightingown

The sound disturbed the peaceful night,
a song we could not recognise.
We looked out at star-freckled skies;
No living creature met our sight.

It sounded like the slap of waves,
Yet somehow not a liquid sound,
More like the wind that prowls around
And through a forest's leafy caves.

But there were neither waves nor trees
Within a score of miles from where
We looked across the little square
Of our backyard and saw the frieze

Of roofs and chimneys and the frail
Scaffolding of ariels;
And then again, like wooden bells
Or distant speech of flapping sail

The curious plainsong could be heard
And, grown accustomed to the dark,
Our eyes at last could just remark
Below our window that strange bird.

It fluttered, hovering near the ground,
Pale and large, its body square
With tiny wings; it trod the air
And danced to its own tuneless sound.

This was a creature of the town
Not found in woods of oak or pine
But on night-hidden washing-line,
The dancing, flapping nightingown.

Vernon Scannell

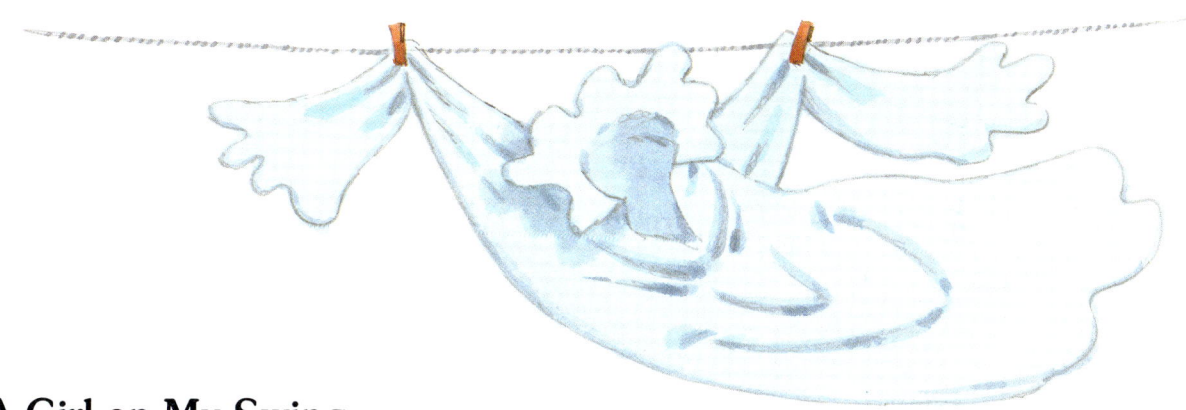

A Girl on My Swing

I saw a girl on my swing
at the top of the garden.
She had yellow hair
with a red ribbon
and all she did was
swing
swing
swing

so I went to her
and asked her
to be my friend
and she said
"I'm not allowed
to have any friends.
My mother says
ghosts
should keep themselves
to themselves."

swing
swing
swing

Sue Stewart

Night Watch

The moon trudged up the wood.
I waited by the wall till everything
was touched with blue, from shadows dark as ink
to sheet-white grass, my clothes too, and my hands,
this time, this one night.

When further and higher up I suddenly heard
steps – stone against stone, a slither. And again,
stone ground on stone again. Heavy. And again –
Hooves? Feet? Paws? Monster's? Or murderer's?

Which way were they going? Coming?
I strained to tell, a bramble – coil hiding me.
No other sound. Which way? This way yet?
Too scared to move at all I turned into a tree,
a dead tree playing statues with the moon.

Whose steps were up there jostling the stones?
They never came or left. Under a little cliff by day
I found them out. Those feet were never legged –
I found water, playing at life in the drips
of a falling streamlet, marking time.

That night, the moon full –
held still by that cold trick, what did I miss?

Libby Houston

26

The Old House

The old house stands at the foot of the hill –
Blackened, silent, still.

> They say on dark nights
> You can hear
> The ghost of a laugh,
> A cry of fear.

That you can see
Beside the wall
A shadowy figure
Gaunt and tall,
Clutching a bundle
Wrapped in a cloak.

That you can see
The swirling smoke
And hear the crackling
Of the fire
And watch as the flames
Leap higher and higher . . .

> The old house stands at the foot of the hill –
> Blackened, silent, still.

John Foster

Haunted Housework

That ghost was such a nuisance
spoiling everyone's demeanour,

until one day and quite by chance,
I whooooooooshed it up in the vacuum cleaner!

Michael Johnson

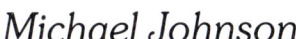

27

Is There a Ghost in This Classroom?

Before anything, don't turn around,
ghosts are never where you expect them to be.
Let's look for signs. Does your desk lid
slam unexpectedly while you're carefully closing it?
Do pens and pencils wriggle and squirm
and slip from your fingers and dive to the floor?
And when you look for them, they've disappeared
and no-one can find them for weeks and weeks
until they turn up under a radiator
looking much the same but not feeling quite right?
Do the legs of your chair wobble nervously?
Do stacks of exercise books mysteriously slither apart
or your biro suddenly start to write in invisible ink?
And when you're working, do you sometimes sense
someone watching you – and it's not the teacher,
who's looking out of the window, or your friends,
who are watching their hands write – but
somewhere you can't see, but can feel like heat or light,
you know something's eyes are staring into you?
Now tell me, do you feel
a sudden small wind licking your ankles,
a slow cold shiver sliding up your leg?
is there an icy itch prickling your neck?
Do you hear a soft whispering, so close and quiet
it sounds like it's inside your head? You do?
Then there is a ghost in this classroom
and it's here
to haunt you.

Dave Calder

28

Witches

Me and Roberta are witches.
She has a really scary witch-dress
made out of a plastic garbage bag
with a place for your head and arms cut out.
I've got a broomstick that is also
a magic wand if I get mad at somebody.
It's still a week until Hallowe'en
but we figure that it's better
to practise being witches for a while
until we get the hang of it.
It's not easy saying witchy things
when you've got a creepy mask
over your mouth with a wart
on the green forehead.
You have to talk crackily and screechily
when putting spells on things.
My brother has a rubber frog and snake
he said I could tie into a necklace
only he won't let me borrow them
until Hallowe'en comes.
Roberta still has to get a witch's hat,
but that's all we need now
unless we find something very frightening
like a realistic fake bat or lizard
before next week.

Julie O'Callaghan

Is It a Monster?

Listen to the beasty
Scratching, scratching.
It's going to bite your feeties
Biting, biting.

While you're gently sleeping
It crawls into your bed
Slides between the soft warm sheets
And SMACKS YOU ON THE HEAD.

You lie quite still
It settles down
You try to scream
It turns around.

Feel its hairy body
Moving, moving.
It crawls along your tummy
Crawling, crawling.

You try to move your body
The beasty gives a grin
You scream and scream and scream and scream
Your mum comes running in.

The light's turned on
The beasty growls
You scream again
Your mother howls.

"HOW MANY TIMES HAVE I TOLD YOU
NOT TO LET THE CAT IN YOUR ROOM!"

Anthony Smith

30

It's Behind You

I don't want to scare you
But just behind you
is a . . .

No! Don't look!
Just act calmly
As if it wasn't there.

Like I said
Can you hear me if I whisper?
Just behind you
Is a . . .

NO! DON'T LOOK!
Just keep on reading
Don't turn round, believe me
It isn't worth it.

If you could see
What I can see standing there
You'd understand.

It's probably one
Of the harmless sort
Although with that mouth
Not to mention the teeth
And all that blood
Dripping down its chin
I wouldn't like to say.

Oh listen
It's trying to speak
I think it wants to be friends.

Oh I see it doesn't, never mind
You'd better leave just in case
I expect you'll escape
if you don't look round.

Oh what a shame!
I thought you'd make it
To the door. Hard luck.
I still think it means no harm
I expect it bites all its friends.

David Harmer

Index of first lines

The publishers wish to thank the following for permission to reproduce the poems in this book: Dave Calder for "The Assembly", "Is There a Ghost in This Classroom?"; Tony Charles for "Under the Bedclothes"; Stanley Cook for "Mary Celeste", "The Ghost"; Gina Douthwaite for "Silas Scale's Piano", "What's There?"; Gavin Ewart for "Creepy"; John Foster for "The Old House", "Who's Afraid?"; David Harmer for "Dracula's Complaint", "It's Behind You"; Libby Houston for "Grandma's Dream", "Night Watch"; Michael Johnson for "Haunted Housework"; Kevin McCann for "The Gloom"; Robin Mellor for "What My Father Said"; Trevor Millum for "Tell Me It Isn't", "Why Are We Hiding?"; Judith Nicholls for "Camping Out", "Fearless", "Willy Was a Wizard"; Julie O'Callaghan for "Witches"; Irene Rawnsley for "Spider Night", "The Follower"; Vernon Scannell for "Dusk Jockey", "Ode to a Nightingown"; Anthony Smith for "Is It a Monster?"; Sue Stewart for "A Girl On My Swing", "The Room Went Cold"; Marian Swinger and Charles Thomson for "The Ancient Horrors". "The Hoover Spook".